Y0-DWN-126

OLIVER AND THE GHOSTS OF BODIE

Written by
Christiane Cassan Wiese with Allen Johnson, Jr.

Illustrated by
Christiane Cassan Wiese

PREMIUM PRESS AMERICA
NASHVILLE, TENNESSEE

Oliver and the Ghosts of Bodie by Christiane Cassan Wiese with Allen Johnson, Jr.

Published by PREMIUM PRESS AMERICA
Printed in Korea

Website **www.allenjohnsonjr.com**

ISBN 1-933725-69-9
Library of Congress Catalog Number 2006902465

PREMIUM PRESS AMERICA gift books are available at special discounts for premiums, sales promotions, fund-raising, or educational use. For details, contact the Publisher at P.O. Box 159015, Nashville, TN 37215, or phone toll free **(800) 891-7323** or **(615) 256-8484**, or fax **(615) 256-8624**.

Website **www.premiumpressamerica.com**

Design by Armour&Armour, Nashville, Tennessee

First Edition March 2006
1 2 3 4 5 6 7 8 9 10

To my most beloved ghosts,
my mother and father
—who transcended parenthood—
and to Jeff, Tony and Oliver
. . . with love.

Introduction

Once upon a time, gold was found in California's Eastern Sierra Mountains. The discovery drew people—including Native Americans—of all colors from all corners of the world. The result was the exciting boomtown of Bodie.

There were good people who came to Bodie, and there were bad people, but all who came were adventurers . . . seeking their fortunes.

These intrepid settlers struggled through scorching hot summers and bitter cold winters on that wind-beaten, barren mountaintop, but when the gold ran out, the people began to leave. A few stayed because, in spite of hardships and disappointments, they loved the little town that had more sky than land. Finally, however, the last old man left, and Bodie became a ghost town.

But far more of the town is left today than a few lovingly preserved structures. If, when you visit Bodie, you bring along your imagination, you will sense up there—surrounded by the vast sky, and eerie, whispering winds—invisible presences from the past. You will know, somehow, that Bodie's spirit never left . . . and perhaps, passing the old schoolhouse, you might meet two young ghosts—a rather solemn Indian girl in a pinafore, and a little Chinese girl with a big smile.

Bodie isn't a place lost in time. For the last thirty years, it has had—and forever will have—a place in my heart!

—Christiane Cassan Wiese—

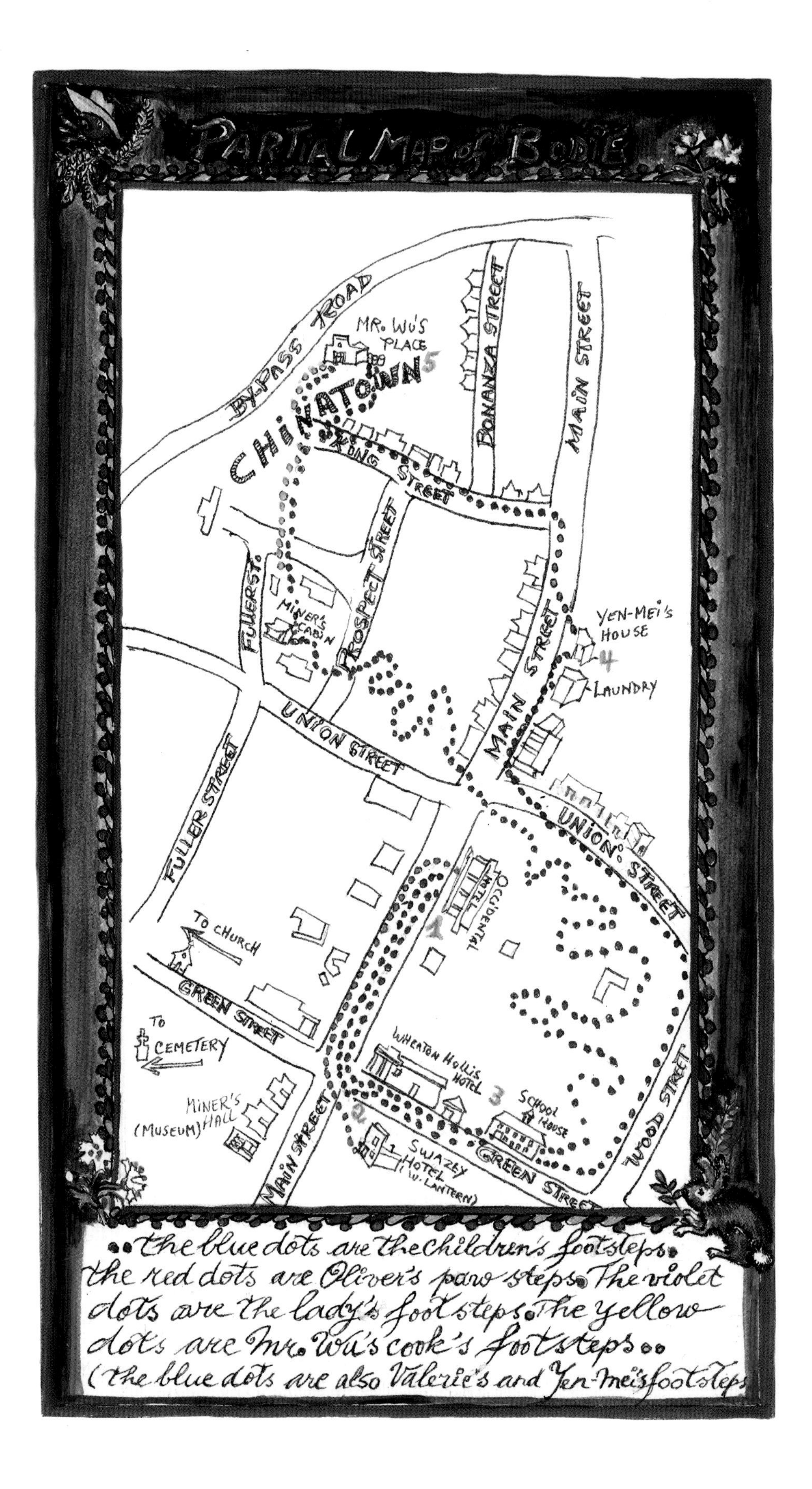
PARTIAL MAP of BODIE
BY-PASS ROAD
MR. WU'S PLACE
5
CHINATOWN
KING STREET
BONANZA STREET
MAIN STREET
FULLER ST.
PROSPECT STREET
MINER'S CABIN
YEN-MEI'S HOUSE
4
LAUNDRY
MAIN STREET
UNION STREET
FULLER STREET
UNION STREET
OCCIDENTAL HOTEL
1
TO CHURCH
GREEN STREET
TO CEMETERY
WHEATON HOLLIS HOTEL
3
SCHOOL HOUSE
WOOD STREET
MINER'S HALL (MUSEUM)
2
MAIN STREET
SWAZEY HOTEL (W. LANTERN)
GREEN STREET
the blue dots are the children's footsteps.
the red dots are Oliver's paw steps. The violet
dots are the lady's footsteps. The yellow
dots are Mr. Wu's cook's footsteps.
(the blue dots are also Valerie's and Yen-Mei's footsteps

Oliver and the Ghosts of Bodie

They named him Oliver Twist because of the twist in his tail and because he— like the Dickens character—was also an orphan.

He was the best of dogs . . . well, almost. Though he was the smartest—he devised his own tricks—and the sweetest—he never growled or showed his teeth—alas, he didn't obey. He failed his final exam in obedience school. Also, he was a wanderer . . . an explorer at heart. He could never resist the call of the wild, and only reluctantly would he come home, because he was loyal to his family and loved them. Above all, Oliver was a lover.

It was summertime and Oliver and his family were headed for the high Sierras in a van packed with fishing rods, tackle boxes, coolers and dog treats. Oliver rode in the back with ten-year-old Tony and his sister Pippa, who was eight. Their parents, Matt and Gwen, took turns driving.

It was a long trip along a mountain range that got higher and higher as they drove north. The rugged mountains and cold mountain air refreshed them after the long drive and, from time to time, Oliver poked his big nose out of the window. Eyes shut and tail wagging, he sniffed the exciting, new wilderness smells. Just as the sun was about to set behind the snow-capped peaks that now surrounded them, they drove into a beautiful valley where placid Angus cattle and graceful horses grazed. In the middle of the valley nestled the little town of Bridgeport.

"Won't be long now, kids," Matt said, causing the children to cheer and bounce on the seat with excitement. Oliver joined in by whining. They drove past the town and through a grove of cottonwood trees whose silver leaves—trembling in the breeze—sounded like thousands of tiny silver bells. They rolled into a golden meadow and finally stopped in front of a small, weathered cabin.

"Let's stretch our legs a bit before we unload," said Gwen.

"Suits me, honey," said Matt. The kids and Oliver were already following a small trail that led across the meadow. When Matt and Gwen caught up, Matt pointed to some faint grooves in the grass.

"See those shallow ruts over there," he said. "They were likely made by wagon wheels. We're probably looking at the old stagecoach road, that went from Carson City to Bodie in the Gold Rush days. Thousands of people came from everywhere to seek their fortunes in the Bodie mines. It didn't last long, though . . . twelve years or so. Eventually Bodie became a ghost town."

"Are there really ghosts in Bodie?" asked Pippa. (One Halloween, when Pippa was little, Tony and his friends had dressed up in sheets and skull masks and scared her out of her wits. Since then, she had been afraid of ghosts.)

"Maybe," Gwen said with a grin, "but chances are we won't be meeting any. Ghosts only come out at night, and we'll be there in the daytime." Pippa was still worried.

"I hope you're right, Mom. Anyway, we won't go near the cemetery, will we? We might see ghosts popping out of their graves."

"What if they do? I'm not afraid of 'em," Tony bragged.

"That's easy for you to say," protested Pippa. "You've never seen a ghost; you've only been one!"

They all laughed and Matt said:

"Some ghosts could be friendly. Have you thought of that?"

"Like me?" Pippa said, looking doubtful.

"Sure, honey," Matt assured her, "they might just be dressed differently and look a bit pale."

"What if you could see through 'em, Dad?" Pippa persisted.

"Well, that might be a bit unnerving. . . ." Matt admitted.

"Could dogs be ghosts?" Tony wondered.

"Why not?" said Matt. "There could be a ghost just like Oliver."

Oliver Twist, who usually perked up when his name was spoken, was too busy sniffing gopher holes to notice.

When they got back to the cabin, Matt and Tony brought in firewood while Gwen started a fire in the wood stove in the kitchen. Pippa unpacked the food.

"Beans and hotdogs tonight, gang," Gwen said, opening a can of beans.

"Yum!" said Tony. "Bring 'em on!"

After dinner, Tony and Pippa unrolled their sleeping bags on the two daybeds in the living room. Oliver curled up next to Tony's bed. After telling the children goodnight, Matt and Gwen retired to the small bedroom. Pippa and Tony were tired and snuggled into their sleeping bags.

"Goodnight, T," came a muffled voice from Pippa's bed.

"Night, Pip," came the sleepy reply.

A horrible shrieking and yowling sound woke Tony, who sat up in his sleeping bag with the hair on his neck prickling. He didn't know that he had heard a pack of coyotes quarreling in the night. The curtain in the window above his bed hadn't been drawn, and a moon was shining in the High Sierra's clear sky. Moonlight flooded the whole cabin. He swung his feet over the side of the bed, expecting them to land on Oliver. They touched the still-warm rug where Oliver had been sleeping. Tony knew at once that the dog was gone. He ran to Pippa's bed and shook her shoulder. She sat up, rubbing the sleep out of her eyes.

"Get up, Pip!" Tony whispered urgently. "Oliver's gone! Quick! Get your clothes on!"

Pippa didn't hesitate. They both knew that Oliver was their responsibility. Matt had been very firm about that when they had adopted him from the Humane Society three years before. Quietly, they pulled their hooded sweatshirts and warm-up pants over their pajamas, got into their socks and tiptoed to the kitchen door, which they found ajar. They sat on the front step and pulled on their boots.

"Come on," whispered Tony, stepping into the crisp night air. They walked around the cabin calling softly, "Oliver . . . Oliver . . . " but he wasn't there. Tony took Pippa's hand, and they started down the trail. Soon they went over a rise in the land and were out of sight of the cabin. Straining his eyes in the moonlight, Tony saw a dark shape near the place where Matt had shown them the old stagecoach road. As they approached, they found Oliver, sitting absolutely still staring into the darkness. One of his ears was up. He was listening intently.

"Hey boy," said Pippa, putting her hand on his head. He gave

a small whine of greeting but continued to stare down the old track, head cocked, listening. Then came the first muffled sound of galloping horses. . . . Soon they saw them. Through the dust, their eyes gleamed white in the cold moonlight. Behind the horses, rocking to a stop was a silvery, shining stagecoach!

The door opened . . . a gloved hand extended and the forefinger curved up . . . beckoning . . . they heard a woman's quavering voice . . .

"Here doggy . . . good doggy . . . come . . . here. . . . "

Oliver, who could never resist an invitation to explore the unknown, jumped in, followed by Tony, who held his collar, and Pippa, who had grabbed his tail. A brief jolt and the coach was once again in motion. Seated by the window was its only passenger—a lady. A small oil lamp in the corner of the coach cast fantastic shadows. It allowed Pippa and Tony to see that the lady was dressed in gray, dusty-looking velvet. She wore a huge black hat topped with gray and white ostrich feathers. Although her face was veiled, she looked quite pretty, but perhaps she had a little too much rouge on her pale cheeks. A wilted bunch of violets was pinned to her shoulder, and the tiny flowers gave off a delicate, distinctive fragrance. The lady smiled and asked:

"What were you children doing out by yourselves in the middle

of nowhere so late at night?"

Reassured by her tone of voice, Tony replied:

"Our dog ran away. We were looking for him."

"Well," the lady said, "it looks like you found him, and now you are on your way to Bodie."

"Isn't Bodie a ghost town?" Pippa asked nervously. The lady laughed.

"Oh sure, I guess you could call it that," the lady replied. "There must be a lot of ghosts hanging around that place."

In a tiny voice, Pippa asked:

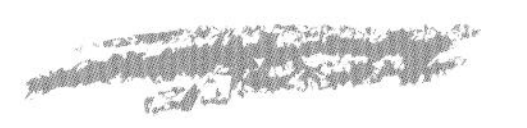

"Are you a ghost?"

Leaning towards her with a mischievous smile the lady said:

"Well, probably so, dearie. After such a journey, I'm sure I look a fright." This time her laughter sounded somewhat sinister, and Pippa, Tony and Oliver huddled closer together.

The stagecoach continued its climb up the dusty, rocky road until finally it started to slow.

"Whoa!" They heard the driver call.

"Bodie, at last!" The woman exclaimed as she straightened her hat and dusted off her sleeves and skirt. She then picked up a large carpetbag and stepped down from the coach. Oliver followed her eagerly, but Tony and Pippa were more hesitant. Under a big, white moon on a barren plateau sprawled a town of small wooden buildings. Everything was dimly lit except for the hotel where the stagecoach had stopped. Pippa pulled on Tony's sleeve and whispered:

"I don't like it here. I'm scared."

"Don't be such a chicken, Pip. Look at Oliver. Dogs can sense danger and he's not scared. His tail is wagging."

"But he always wags his tail. . . . " said Pippa, unconvinced.

Their traveling companion, for her part, wasn't the least bit frightened. With the feathers of her hat dancing wildly in the wind, she was patting one of the horses and joking with the stagecoach driver. The children looked at the rundown hotel with its two large, flickering kerosene lanterns on either side of the entrance. Tony turned to Pippa.

"Wait here, Pip. I'll go in and find out how we can get back."

Holding Oliver by the collar he climbed the weary, creaky stairs and took one cautious step into the lobby. Under an imposing chandelier, a guest clerk with carefully pomaded hair was scribbling something in the register. There were several guests idling away their time. Some wore pistols in low-slung holsters. Their dusty boots sprawled over the worn carpet, and their unshaven faces looked either gloomy, fierce or both. They looked him over coldly, but Tony tried his best to ignore them. He kept his eyes riveted on the hotel clerk. He swallowed hard and mustered his courage to speak.

"Excuse me, sir, can you tell me when the next stagecoach for Bridgeport will be leaving tonight?" As he spoke, he could see the look of disbelief coming over the clerk's face. There was a brief, stunned silence followed by a thundering roar of laughter from around the room. By the door, sitting alarmingly close to where Tony and Oliver were standing, there was a grubby character with red, bushy, ferocious eyebrows and matching mustache who slapped his thighs so noisily while he laughed that he made Oliver jump.

"Hey, kid! You're shore funny, and you dress even funnier, but I shore like them boots. Where'd you git 'em? Too bad they ain't my size." Tony felt cold and hollow in his stomach. At this point, the desk clerk, who had laughed along with the others, began to feel sorry for the frightened boy. While carefully wiping his pince-nez, he said gently:

"Sorry, son, but you won't be going anywhere out of Bodie tonight. There won't be another stage for three or four days."

Fighting rising tears, Tony managed a polite "thank

AURORA-BODIE
BODIE STANDARD

you" and hurried back to Pippa, who was standing quite alone outside. Knowing now that the hotel was not the kind of place where they could get help, Tony, Pippa, and Oliver instinctively turned to their first acquaintance, the mysterious lady who was now chatting away with some passerby. The children approached her, but just as they were about to ask her advice, she gave them a bright, vague little smile, patted their cheeks and walked briskly away. Not knowing what else to do, the children and Oliver followed her on the rough, wooden sidewalk until the musketeer hat and the dusty velvet suit disappeared under a large ornate lantern into a narrow house. The door closed firmly in their faces, and all the windows were shuttered. Feeling lost and bewildered, the children looked around and saw a variety of buildings . . . some high, some low. The shops, saloons and boarding houses had false fronts. Shadows moved around behind foggy windows. They heard loud voices, laughter, singing and some piano and banjo music. The wind had picked up and was moaning and sighing through the buildings, adding to the eerie feeling of the strange world that surrounded them. Tony felt Pippa's little hand sliding into his, and he was grateful. Although he was a boy and older than Pippa, he was beginning to feel ever so small and frightened. Oliver, too, felt comforted by Pippa's hand clinging to his collar.

They were now in front of a rather large and handsome building. In the smoky glow of a kerosene lamp in one of the second-floor windows, they could see the silhouette of a lady writing at a desk. Behind the ground-floor windowpanes, they could just make out rows of small desks.

"It's the town schoolhouse," Tony said.

"Someone there will help us," Pippa said.

Peering in, they saw a partly open door to the right of the blackboard. A thin ray of light shined through from the room beyond.

"Maybe there's someone there besides the lady upstairs," Pippa said. Oliver wagged his tail in agreement.

"Come on," said Tony, leading them around the back of the building. They found a door with light showing through the crack at the bottom. They opened it and saw a small kitchen with a young girl reading at a table beside a cast-iron stove. She stood

HOTEL

up and smiled in greeting.

She was taller than them and darker. She must have been twelve years old. She wore a faded calico dress under an outgrown, faded gray pinafore.

"Who are you?" she asked. "What are you doing out so late?"

"I'm Tony, this is my sister, Pippa and this is our dog, Oliver Twist. We're staying in a cabin near Bridgeport. After we went to bed, Oliver got out and ran away. We found him, but when a stagecoach came, we got in and found ourselves in Bodie. It was like a dream. It still is. Are you real?" The girl only smiled at this.

“We don’t know how to get back,” Tony continued. “We need help.”

“You better come in. You must be awfully cold,” the girl said. She sounded kind and sympathetic.

“My name is Valerie. Miss Pettigrew, our schoolteacher, adopted me. I am a Piute Indian and an orphan. Miss Pettigrew named me Valerie because we Indians must have names that mean something. Valerie means ‘courageous.’ ”

Pippa said:

“You look like a girl in one of my books, *The Little House on the Prairie*. You’re dressed just like her.” Valerie looked at her with widened eyes and said:

“I don’t know that book, but I’ve never seen anyone with clothes like yours. You must have come from some faraway place. . . . ”

“Or time,” muttered Tony.

While they were talking, Oliver slipped quietly out through the door. An intriguing smell led him to a group of sage bushes and then to another group and yet another. Soon he was well out in the wilderness. Back inside, Tony gave a start.

“Oliver! Where is Oliver?”

"Oh, no, not again!" cried Pippa. They both looked a Valerie.

"We must look for him right away. Miss Pettigrew still has many homework papers to correct, so I won't be missed. I'll help you find him. I'll just get my shawl and lantern first." As soon as she left the room, Pippa whispered:

"Do you think she's a ghost?"

"She must be," Tony answered, "but isn't she nice?"

Pippa agreed. "Yes, she is . . . and not at all spooky. Dad was right; some ghosts can be really friendly."

In the meantime, sniffing and exploring, Oliver Twist had slowly made his way towards the miners' quarters. On the way, he had stopped when his inquisitive nose detected a fascinating, gamy smell. Sure enough, a couple of large, strange-looking birds emerged from the brush. They were sage grouse. Oliver was extremely fond of birds. At home, napping by the bird feeder, he'd become their protector. Sparrows, robins and mourning doves felt safe in his company because they knew that the neighborhood cats wouldn't dare to come prowling in his territory.

The two grouse passed right under Oliver's nose, their heads bobbing up and down in a silly way. As they strutted away, a handsome newcomer appeared on the scene. He looked somewhat like a dog, very slender in the waist, with a wild look in his golden slanted eyes. His beautiful, pale, silky coat shimmered in

the moonlight. Oliver had never seen a coyote before. Was it a ghost dog? The coyote didn't seem alarmed by Oliver's presence. He must have sensed the dog was not a threat. He stood still, softly waving his elegant fan-like tail back and forth, and Oliver responded, happily wagging his own curly one. But to Oliver's disappointment, his new acquaintance—after giving him a backward glance—quickly left in pursuit of the two scatterbrained birds that could be heard foolishly clucking away in some nearby bushes. Oliver, who had hoped to make a new friend, resumed his exploring with a whine of disappointment. He passed some dingy shacks and noisy, smoky saloons and finally reached an isolated house with a big sign on top of its tin roof that read "Black Hawk Mining Company." Above the door, swinging in the wind, another smaller sign said "Office." There was a porch in front where two miners were seated in rocking chairs. One was young and the other was old. The men looked terribly shabby. They wore battered, shapeless hats, dirty, collarless shirts with frayed cuffs and threadbare trousers held up by faded red suspenders. Nonetheless, they were friendly.

"You look awful thirsty, pooch," said the old miner. He filled an empty bean can with water and chuckled. "Here . . .
have one on us," he said, putting the can down on the ground. Oliver gratefully lapped the water up and then, leaving the two

men to their whiskey, he trotted into the darkness.

He felt a sharp pain from a thorn in one of his paws, and he knew now he was lost. He had to find his way back to Pippa and Tony. Relying on his large, sensitive nose as a compass, he began to retrace his paw prints, stopping at times to listen for any unusual sounds in the darkness around him. Suddenly, he thought he heard something! He could sense danger. Just as he tensed himself to run, two strong hands grabbed him from behind. He felt long fingernails digging sharply into his back.

Meanwhile, Pippa, Tony and Valerie had been desperately searching for him. All three called, "Oliver . . . Oliver . . . " at regular intervals. All was in vain. They were becoming extremely worried. Valerie said:

"I'm afraid Oliver might have wandered into Chinatown."

"Chinatown?" cried Pippa, and Tony asked:

"Don't Chinese eat dogs?" Valerie, trying her best to reassure them, said:

"Not many do, really." Realizing how terrified her new friends were she quickly added, "My best friend, Yen-mei, is Chinese. She's very clever, and she'll help us. I'm sure she will." It was scary to go into that part of town, but Valerie seemed determined to prove herself worthy of her given name and her Indian ancestry. So, holding her lantern high with Pippa on one side and Tony on the other, she bravely led the way to Chinatown.

When they got there, in spite of the late hour, they saw that all the shops had flickering little oil lamps in their windows. Bright-colored paper lanterns hung above doorways. Valerie whispered:

"That smell is opium. It gives weird dreams to those who smoke it. It's bad! Very bad!"

They hurried until finally they reached a laundry shop. They looked in and saw

people busy ironing amid crisscrossing clothes lines. In the center of the room there was a large pot-bellied stove where irons and teapots were kept steaming hot. Just past the laundry there was a small frame house. Valerie knocked on a dark, low window, and a small, heart-shaped face appeared.

"It's Yen-mei," she whispered to Pippa and Tony, motioning urgently for the girl to come out. After a few minutes, a tiny girl with a big smile stood in front of Valerie, Pippa and Tony. She was holding a lantern. She was dressed in the traditional Chinese costume: a blue quilted cotton jacket over matching cotton trousers. Her thick, shiny black bangs stopped just short of her almond-shaped eyes, and her hair was pulled back in a single braid. Valerie spoke quickly:

"Yen-mei, these are my friends, Tony and Pippa. They have an emergency. Their dog Oliver Twist is lost. He could be somewhere in Chinatown. We need your help and advice." Yen-mei's face became serious.

"If he is here, there is only one big danger: Mr. Wu! We Chinese of Bodie do not eat dogs. They are our pets. But

Mr. Wu would! He is evil! He sells opium and he has a cook with disgusting yellow teeth and long, dirty black fingernails who keeps in his kitchen a collection of the scariest looking knives. . . ." Seeing the horrified look on both Tony's and Pippa's faces, Valerie interrupted her.

"Yes, yes, we understand, but what do you think we ought to do?" Yen-mei frowned as she considered the problem, then her face brightened.

"I have a plan," she said. "Follow me to Mr. Wu's and when we get there, do exactly what I tell you."

When they reached their frightful destination, Yen-mei took them to the side of the house and told them to hide behind some barrels that were stored alongside the wall and wait for her. In the dark, with faint hearts, they heard the incongruously cheery sound of chimes as Yen-mei pushed open the door of Mr. Wu's sinister shop. Yen-mei was not only brave; she was also very smart. In the dimly lit entrance she immediately spotted Oliver Twist looking miserable in a large bamboo cage by the counter. Yen-mei smiled at him and winked as if to say, "Be quiet. I'm your

friend. I'm here to help you." Oliver seemed to understand. He flattened himself out like a pancake, but his eyes followed her every move. The infamous Mr. Wu was in the kitchen in the back of the store having a heated argument in Chinese with his cook. The discussion was all about frying as opposed to stewing. Mr. Wu complained bitterly:

"A stew takes too long! The last time you made one, my distinguished guests and I waited three and a half hours for your stupid concoction. Cut him into pieces, mince him or whatnot and, for heaven's sake, fry him! With ginger, onion, soy sprouts, cabbage, whatever—but fry him!" Rubbing his bony hands, the cook retorted:

"Eminent master, if you permit your abject, humble servant to speak, stewing would be by far the most delectable choice. Tender juicy morsels of this dog would melt in the mouths of your honorable guests, and their praises would go up so high they would reach the most glorious and venerable of your infinitely respected ancestors." Oliver didn't understand this gruesome exchange, but Yen-mei caught every word. Yet, managing a smile, she bravely walked up to these potential cannibals and, with just a slight tremor in her voice, asked:

"Would Mr. Wu like to have his laundry delivered tomorrow?" Mr. Wu was massive and towered over little Yen-mei. He was dressed in black brocade pajamas and wore a black and red skull cap. A long, thin gray braid hung down between his massive shoulders. He grumbled:

"Of course I do, you silly goose. Now, off with you!" Turning away, he resumed his shouting at the cook. That scrawny fellow looked exactly as Yen-mei had described him earlier. His sinister smile revealed dingy yellow teeth. His nervously fluttering hands displayed long black fingernails. He stood next to a butcher's block on which arrays of wicked-looking knives were lined up for their grim purpose. Their angry debate continued on how to prepare and cook poor Oliver. Yen-mei hurried back toward the entrance, unlatching the bamboo cage as she passed. Ever so quietly, Oliver slipped out of his prison and followed her. They rejoined the fearful trio hidden behind the barrels. Then they all broke into a wild, breathless run to Yen-mei's house. Pippa collapsed on the steps. With her knees clasped to her chest and her little red head hanging down, she sobbed:

"I want to go back to Mom and Dad." Tony put his arm around her shoulders.

"Me too," he said quietly. A panting and rather sheepish Oliver Twist leaned his big black nose on Pippa's shoulder in silent, whole-hearted agreement. Yen-mei spoke up with a very firm voice.

"We'll get you back, all right. I'll wake up my brother Cheng. As soon as he can get our mules harnessed up to the wagon, he'll take you back to where you came from. Meanwhile, you can't stay here. It's too dangerous. Mr. Wu might come looking for Oliver. Take them to the schoolhouse, Valerie. They'll be safe there until Cheng comes." With a big grin, she pulled a piece of rope out of her pocket and tied it to Oliver's collar. As she kissed the top of his head, she said, "There now, he can't run away again." With everyone smiling at him and patting him, Oliver Twist knew he was forgiven. Wagging his tail as usual, he was once again his old happy self.

When they got back to the schoolhouse, they saw that Miss Pettigrew was still working upstairs. Valerie served them hot cocoa and cookies in the cozy kitchen, and Oliver lapped up a large bowl of milk. Then they all went into the classroom to wait on the wagon. Smiling, Valerie went to the blackboard and wrote: "Pippa, Yen-mei, Tony, Oliver and Valerie are friends forever!" Just as she finished, Yen-mei arrived with her brother Cheng, a tall, lanky boy with a smile as big as his sister's. After Valerie introduced him to Tony, Pippa and Oliver, Cheng said:

"We're lucky. Tonight there's a full moon. I can take you back right now."

It was time to say goodbye. There were tears in everyone's eyes. Pippa put her arms around Valerie and Yen-mei and said:

"Valerie is right. We are friends forever! We'll never forget you. Never!" In a choked voice, Tony added:

"Never!"

Oliver agreed by tenderly licking his two rescuers' noses. They all laughed. Cheng picked up the reins as Pippa, Oliver and Tony climbed into the back of the wagon. As they drove out of the town,

Tony and Pippa waved and waved to Valerie and Yen-mei, who stood together with their lanterns holding hands until, as Bodie gradually faded away into darkness, they became just two tiny flickering lights, no bigger than fireflies.

The bright moon lit the Sierra landscape from its rocky peaks down to the glittering waters of Mono Lake and the strange anthills of its salty shores. Cheng drove down the dusty road until he finally reached the very spot where the phantom stagecoach had stopped for them earlier that night. After thanking Cheng and waving him and his mules goodbye, Tony and Pippa, with Oliver leading the way, ran up the little trail to the cabin. The moon still lighted the living room where they shed their sweatshirts, warm-up pants, socks and hiking boots. Behind the bedroom door, totally unaware of their children's extraordinary journey into the past, Matt and Gwen were peacefully sleeping. Tony whispered:

"Not a word of what happened tonight to anyone. Promise?" And Pippa whispered back: "Promise!"

As for Oliver Twist, he couldn't possibly have been made to swear to anything. The adventurous night had taken its toll. He lay by Tony's feet with his nose between his paws, sound asleep.

They were all up bright and early the next morning. Gwen noticed that Pippa, Tony and Oliver seemed tired. She assured them it was the altitude.

"It affects some people more than others," she said. "You'll get used to it after awhile, and you won't feel it anymore." Matt came in and sat down at the table.

"Okay, everybody!" he announced cheerfully. "We're going to Bodie today."

"Bodie! Oh, no," cried Pippa and Tony. Oliver Twist, who was telepathic, ducked under the table.

"What's the matter with you three this morning?" asked Matt "No, don't tell me it's the altitude. I won't have it. Bodie's the greatest ghost town in the West. We're going to see it, and that's that." And so they did.

In the bright sunshine Bodie seemed small and deserted to Tony, Pippa and Oliver. Here and there they saw some old, crooked houses with torn curtains behind their broken windows. There were collapsing, weather-beaten stables and barns, tiny leaning outhouses without doors and abandoned wagons. (One looked just like Cheng's.) Most of the wagons were missing their wheels. The splitting, sun-dried planks that had once been sidewalks, the broken-down mining equipment, old tin cans and

other debris scattered among the sagebrush, were all remnants of a long-gone way of life.

Gwen had been studying the town map and said:

"Why don't we see if we can find Chinatown?"

At the mention of the word, Tony thought of the vile Mr. Wu, and Oliver, who could read minds, started shaking like a leaf.

"Now what's the matter with that dog?" asked Matt, impatiently pulling on the leash. "Come on! Let's go!" But Oliver would not budge.

"Oh, let him be," said Gwen. "The poor thing hasn't been himself today. And besides, the sun is awfully hot for him, and from what I read, there isn't anything left of Chinatown. Why don't we have a look at that lovely old schoolhouse instead and find a place where Oliver can lie down and cool off?" And soon, with Matt and Gwen by his side, Oliver rested in the shade of the building. A blissful breeze had replaced the haunting wind of the night before. His eyes were now fixed on Tony and Pippa, who were standing on some tree stumps peering through the hazy windowpanes of the schoolhouse. In the classroom were the little desks with the hard wooden seats where they had sat waiting for Yen-mei and Cheng. Everything was covered with gray dust. Through thick cobwebs, they saw the blackboard, and holding their breath, they read what was written on it: PIPPA, YEN-MEI, TONY, OLIVER AND VALERIE ARE FRIENDS FOREVER. Exchanging knowing smiles, the children went back to their parents and Oliver. As they all headed back through the town, they passed a small, lopsided house with a broken lantern hanging crookedly above the narrow, boarded-up front door. Oliver, Pippa and Tony became aware of a delicate but persistent scent.

"Violets!" cried Pippa. "Just like the ones that. . . . " But she felt Tony's nudge and put her hand quickly over her mouth.

"Violets in Bodie?" said Gwen, laughing. "Really darling, you do have such an imagination. Sage. That would be more likely, don't you think?" She looked at Matt. "I think it's time to leave Bodie to its ghosts and rejoin the living in Bridgeport."

As they drove away, Pippa, Tony and Oliver turned around to look back. They saw—standing on a slope just where the town began—two slender figures: one taller, dressed in faded calico; the other smaller, in dark blue Chinese pajamas. Both had their arms outstretched in a farewell gesture. Then some tumbleweed rolled by in a cloud of dust and the figures vanished, taking Bodie with them. . . .

Pippa was never again afraid of ghosts. One is only afraid of what one does not know. Pippa and Tony never forgot Valerie, Yen-mei, Cheng and the strange lady with her violets. Nor did they forget the evil Mr. Wu and his sinister cook. They remembered the long-dead, old mining town that mysteriously came back to life just for them. One day

they planned to tell their parents what happened that night in the Sierras but not yet. Grown-ups have secrets that they cannot share with children, but children have their own secrets that grown-ups wouldn't understand.

Dogs too have memories, and that is why they dream. Oliver Twist often dreamt of that extraordinary ride in the ghostly stagecoach bound for Bodie. He remained a wanderer with a particular fondness for abandoned dirt roads. And if ever one could be found on a night of full moon, you would find him sitting very erect, one ear up, eyes shut, his big black leathery nose eagerly sniffing the air for the scent of violets, and his adventurous heart yearning—with perhaps slight apprehension but such fervent hope—that a stagecoach would once again appear.

THE END